For Raymond

THE WITCH BABY
WENDY SMITH

PUFFIN BOOKS

Wanda the witch baby was about to cast her first spell.

"I will make the rain stop and the sun shine — just like Mother does," she thought.

But although she had used the freshest frogs,
the spell did not work.

"Or perhaps I'll try flying, just like Father does."

And although she did everything she had seen her father do, the flight was not a success.

"Maybe it would help if I had a cat," Wanda thought.

But the cat made no difference.

"We'll go and ask Granny about spells and flying," she said to the cat. "I'd better leave a note for Mother and Father, and then tidy myself up for Granny. I must file my nails and polish my stars."

Wanda and the cat were just leaving when the next-door wizard came out of his house carrying a broom.

"Hello, Wanda, where are you off to?" he asked.

"I'm going to Granny's."

"Well, I'm flying that way and I'll drop you off at the corner where your grandmother's coven meets. Hop on!"

And off they flew.

The sky was unusually crowded,

and the wizard found it hard steering through all the traffic.

They had nearly reached Granny's when a wicked witch, flying too fast, crashed into them. Luckily no one was hurt.

"I know a spell to deal with you," said Wanda boldly — planning to turn the witch into a worm.

Wanda cast the spell and there was a splendid puff of smoke. But then a strange, unwormlike creature appeared.

"That's not what I had in mind," said Wanda as the peculiar creature galloped off. "But it's far more interesting!"

The wizard flew on and dropped Wanda off near Granny's house. "Wanda dear!" cried Granny. "You're just in time for tea and toasted toads."

After tea, Wanda played with Granny's bats and spiders.
"Tell me, Granny," she said, "have you any tips on flying? And what's the best spell to turn a wicked witch into a worm? And how do you make the sun shine?"

"Broom flying is beyond your years," said Granny wisely. "And wicked witches are best left alone. As for weather spells, they are rarely worth the trouble. But let me tell you a simple, foolproof spell you may care to try."

Wanda was very glad she had come to see Granny.
"Thank you for the tea and all your help," she said. "And now please do your going-home spell."
In no time at all Wanda and the cat were spinning home.

"I am about to cast a simple and foolproof spell," she announced to her parents who were busy catching snakes at the bottom of the garden. "Please join me for a short walk."

So Wanda and her parents walked to a place high on a hill in the woods.

And when it was dark enough Wanda whispered, beneath her breath, the simple and foolproof spell that her grandmother had taught her.

"Come out, come out all you animals with tails — and dance!"

But not one animal appeared.

Instead, Wanda had made the moon turn pink.

"That was not quite what I had planned," said Wanda as they walked home, "but it's a much prettier spell."

"What a clever witch baby," said Wanda's father, tucking her up in bed that evening. "What will you try tomorrow?"

"Tell us," said her mother as she kissed her little witch baby goodnight, "how did you make the moon turn pink?"

But Wanda was already fast asleep and dreaming…

…she had made a spell turn out perfectly. She had made the biggest, most delicious tea in the world — even tastier than Granny's toasted toads.

1989